The Adventures of Huckleberry Finn

*Retold from the Mark Twain
original by Oliver Ho*

Illustrated by Dan Andreasen

STERLING CHILDREN'S BOOKS
New York

STERLING CHILDREN'S BOOKS
New York

An Imprint of Sterling Publishing Co., Inc.
1166 Avenue of the Americas
New York, NY 10036

STERLING CHILDREN'S BOOKS and the distinctive Sterling Children's Books logo are
trademarks of Sterling Publishing Co., Inc.

Design by Renato Stanisic

Classic Starts is a trademark of Sterling Publishing Co., Inc.

ISBN 978-1-4027-2499-2

Library of Congress Cataloging-in-Publication Data
Ho, Oliver.
  The adventures of Huckleberry Finn / retold from the Mark Twain original ;
abridged by Oliver Ho ; illustrated by Dan Andreasen; afterword by Arthur Pober.
    p. cm.—(Classic starts)
Summary: An abridged version of the adventures of a nineteenth-century boy and
a runaway slave as they float down the Mississippi River on a raft.
  ISBN 1-4027-2499-3
[1. Voyages and travels—Fiction. 2. Mississippi River—History—19th century—Fiction. 3.
Slavery—Fiction. 4. Friendship—Fiction.] I. Andreasen, Dan, ill. II. Twain, Mark, 1835–1910.
Adventures of Huckleberry Finn. III. Title. IV. Series.

PZ7.H63337Adv 2006
[Fic]—dc222005015837

                                                          2005015837

Distributed in Canada by Sterling Publishing Co., Inc.
c/o Canadian Manda Group, 664 Annette Street
Toronto, Ontario, Canada M6S 2C8
Distributed in the United Kingdom by GMC Distribution Services,
Castle Place, 166 High Street, Lewes, East Sussex, England BN7 1XU
Distributed in Australia by Capricorn Link (Australia) Pty. Ltd.
P.O. Box 704, Windsor, NSW 2756, Australia

For information about custom editions, special sales, and premium and corporate purchases,
please contact Sterling Special Sales at 800-805-5489 or specialsales@sterlingpublishing.com.

Manufactured in China
Lot#:
16 18 20 19 17
08/16

www.sterlingpublishing.com

CONTENTS

ᥱ᧒

CHAPTER 1

Scene: The Mississippi Valley
Forty to fifty years ago (1835–1845)

Tom and the Widow

‿∽

You don't know about me unless you've read a book called *The Adventures of Tom Sawyer*, but that doesn't matter. That book was written by Mr. Mark Twain and he told the truth, mainly. There were some things he stretched, though. That's nothing. I've never met anyone who hasn't lied at one time or another, except Aunt Polly, or the widow. That's Tom's Aunt Polly. She and the Widow Douglas are both in that book, which is mostly a true book, as I said before.

The way that book ends, Tom and I found the

money that the robbers had hidden in the cave and it made us rich. Six thousand dollars each, all in gold. Judge Thatcher put it in the bank for us and we could each get a dollar a day. We didn't know what to do with all that money anyway. The Widow Douglas took me in as a son and promised to civilize me.

It was rough living in the house all the time. The widow was so regular and decent in all of her ways. When I couldn't stand it any longer, I ran away. I got into my old rags and felt free and satisfied. But Tom Sawyer hunted me down and said he was planning to start a gang, a band of robbers. He said I might join in if I went back to the widow and acted properly. So I went back.

The widow cried over me and called me a poor lost lamb. She called me a lot of other names, too, but she never meant any harm. She put me in some new clothes again and I couldn't do anything but sweat and feel all cramped up.

Then the old things started up again. The widow rang a bell for supper and I had to come in on time. When I got to the table I couldn't start eating right away. I had to wait for the widow to lower her head and grumble a little over the food. There was nothing wrong with the food, except that everything was separate. I was used to eating a stew full of odds and ends. Things in a stew get mixed up and the juice kind of swaps around and everything goes better.

The widow's sister, Miss Watson, had just come to live with her. She set after me on my first night back with a spelling-book. She worked with me for about an hour, until the widow made her ease up. I couldn't stand it much longer.

I went up to my room, sat by the window, and tried to think of something cheerful, but it was no use. I got so down-hearted and lonesome I wished I had some company. Pretty soon I heard a twig snap down in the dark. I sat still and listened. I could just barely hear a *"me-yow! me-yow!"*

I said, *"me-yow! me-yow!"* as softly as I could and then I put out the light and climbed out of the window onto the shed. I slipped down to the ground and crawled in among the trees. And sure enough, there was Tom waiting for me.

We went along a short path. Just as we passed the kitchen, I fell over a root and made a noise. We crouched down and laid still. Miss Watson's slave, Jim, was sitting at the kitchen door.

"Who's there?" he said.

He listened some more and walked near us. For minutes and minutes there wasn't a sound. He couldn't see us, but he must have known someone was nearby. He sat down on the ground near me and Tom and said he knew someone was there. He told us he would wait until we showed ourselves. He leaned against a tree and stretched his legs out until one of them

almost touched mine. Soon he began to breathe heavily and then he started snoring, so Tom and I could finally get away.

When Tom and I got to the edge of the hilltop, we looked down into the village and could see three or four lights twinkling. The stars over us were sparkling. Down by the village was the river. It was a whole mile wide and awfully still and grand. We found Jo Harper and Ben Rogers, and two or three more of the boys. We untied a little boat, floated down the river to the big scar on the hillside, and went ashore.

We went to a clump of bushes, where Tom made everybody swear to keep the place a secret. Then he showed us a hole in the hill, right in the thickest part of the bushes. We lit candles and crawled in on our hands and knees. After a minute or two the cave opened up. Tom ducked under a wall in the cave and crawled into another hole. We followed along the narrow path until we got into a kind of room, all damp and sweating and cold.

Tom said:

"Now, we'll start this band of robbers and call it Tom Sawyer's Gang. Everybody that wants to join has got to take an oath."

We were willing so Tom got out a sheet of paper with the oath written on it. It swore every boy to stick to the gang and never tell any of its secrets. If anybody ever did anything wrong to any boy in the band, one of the other boys would be ordered to get even with that person and his family and he would have to do it.

Everybody said it was a great oath and asked Tom if he made it up himself. He said some of it, but the rest was out of pirate-books and robber-books. He told us that every important gang had an oath like it.

"Wait, Huck Finn doesn't have a family," Ben

Rogers said. "How could we get even with him if he doesn't have a family? What are you going to do about him?"

"Well, doesn't he have a father?" Tom asked.

"Yes, but you can't ever find him these days. He used to get in a lot of trouble around town, but he hasn't been seen in these parts for a year or more."

They talked it over and they weren't going to let me in the gang. Nobody could think of anything to do. I was almost ready to cry, but all at once I thought of a way. I offered them Miss Watson. They could get even with her if they wanted. That satisfied everyone and they let me in.

Then Tom told us we would be highwaymen.

"We'll stop stagecoaches and carriages on the road. We'll wear masks and take people's watches and money. We'll bring some of the people to the cave here and keep them until they're ransomed."

"Ransomed? What's that?" asked Ben Rogers.

"I don't know," Tom said. "But that's what they do. I've seen it in books, so of course that's what we've got to do."

"But how can we do it if we don't know what it is?"

"Well, we've just got to do it," Tom said. "Didn't I tell you it's in the books? Do you want to do things differently from the books and get things all messed up?"

"That's fine to say," said Ben. "But how are these people going to be ransomed if we don't know how to do it to them?"

"Well, I don't know," Tom said. "Maybe if we keep them until they're ransomed it means we keep them here a long, long time."

"Now that's something," Ben said. "Why couldn't you say that before? We'll keep them until they're ransomed, a good long time. Boy, that'll be bothersome. They'll be eating up everything and always trying to get loose."

"How could they get loose if there's a guard watching over them?" Tom asked.

"A guard? Well, that is good," Ben said. "So somebody's got to sit up all night and never get any sleep, just to watch them. I think that's foolish. I don't see why we have to do that."

"Because it's in the books, that's why," Tom said. "Now, Ben, do you want to do things the right way or not? Don't you think the people who made the books know the right ways to do things? Do you think you can teach them anything? Not at all. No sir, we'll just go on and ransom them in the regular way."

Little Tommy Barnes was asleep by now and when they woke him up he was scared and started to cry. He said he wanted to go home to his ma. He didn't want to be a robber anymore. They all made fun of him for that, which made him mad, and he said he would tell everyone our secrets. Tom gave him five cents to keep quiet and said we would meet again next week to plan our first robberies.

After the walk home, I climbed back up the shed and crept into my window just before dawn. My new clothes were all greased up and covered with clay and I was dog-tired.

CHAPTER 2

A Bad Sign

As the boys had said, my pap hadn't been seen for more than a year, and that was fine by me. I didn't want to see him ever again. He used to get angry with me and cuff me with the back of his hand, though I used to hide in the woods most of the time when he was around. Some people even said he had died, but I didn't believe them. I believed the old man would turn up again. But I wished he wouldn't.

The boys and I played robbers now and then for about a month. Then I quit. All the boys did.

We hadn't robbed anybody, only pretended. We used to hop out of the woods and go charging down on people in carts who were taking plants and animals to market. But we never robbed any of them. Tom called the hogs "gold treasure," and he called the turnips and stuff "jewelry," and we would go to the cave and talk about what we had done. I just couldn't see any profit in it.

Three or four months passed and it was well into the winter now. I had been to school. I could spell and read and write a little, and could say the multiplication table up to six times seven is thirty-five. I didn't think I could get higher than that if I lived forever.

At first I hated the school, but by and by I found I could stand it. Whenever I got too tired of it I played hooky. The trouble that would bring the next day cheered me up. I was getting sort of used to the widow's ways, too, and they weren't so hard on me. Living in a house and sleeping in a bed were still a little uncomfortable. Before the cold weather came I would slip out and sleep in the woods sometimes, and that was restful for me. I liked the old ways best, but I was beginning to like the new ones a little bit, too. The widow said I was coming along and doing well. She said she wasn't ashamed of me.

One morning I happened to knock over the salt shaker at breakfast, which was bad luck. It made me terribly nervous and worried. I felt so bad that I had to go for a walk to try and figure out how to keep off the bad luck. I knew something would happen.

I went down to the front garden and climbed over a fence. There was an inch of new snow on the ground and I saw somebody's footprints. This person had come up from the quarry and stood around for a while. Then he went back around the garden fence. It was strange that he hadn't come in or knocked on the door after standing around like that. I was curious. I was going to follow the tracks, but then I bent down to look at them closer. There was a cross in the left boot-heel made with big nails, a sign to keep off the devil. It was something I recognized from my pap's shoes.

I started running as fast as I could. I looked over my shoulder every now and then, but I didn't see anybody. I was at Judge Thatcher's as quickly as I could get there. He asked if I had come for some of the money he was keeping for me.

"No, sir," I said. "I don't want it at all. I want you to take it. I want to give it to you—the six thousand and everything else."

He looked surprised and couldn't seem to figure it out.

"Please take it," I said. "And don't ask me anything. Then I won't have to tell any lies."

It took some convincing. At last he made me sign a piece of paper. He said it would mean I had given him all of my money and property.

Then I left to find Miss Watson's slave, Jim, who had some magic items that were supposed to be able to tell the future. He knew all about good and bad luck. I told Jim that my pap was here again and that I had found his tracks in the snow. I wanted to know what he was going to do and how long he was going to stay.

Jim took an old hairball that that had come from a bull, which he said was supposed to be magic. It was as big as a fist. Jim said it had a spirit inside. He shook it, listened to it, and dropped it on the floor. He did this again and again, and then he put his ear against it to listen. He said it wouldn't talk without money.

I had an old fake quarter and asked if the hairball could tell the difference. Jim said it probably couldn't, so we cleaned up my quarter and put it underneath the hairball. He listened to it one more time and said it was ready to tell my fortune.

"Your old father doesn't know yet what he's going to do," Jim said. "Sometimes he thinks he'll go away and then he thinks he'll stay. The best is to rest easy and let the old man make his own way. But you are all right. You're going to have great trouble in your life, and great joy. Sometimes you're going to get hurt and sometimes you're going to get sick, but every time you're going to get well again. You should keep away from water as much as you can. And don't take any risks."

I left feeling a little better, but still mighty nervous. Well I didn't have to wait too long. When I lit my candle and went up to my room that night, there sat my pap!

I shut the door and when I turned around, there he was. I used to be scared of him all the time, because of how badly he treated me. I guess I was a little scared right then, too. But after I got

over the surprise of seeing him so suddenly, I realized I wasn't scared of him very much at all.

He was almost fifty and he looked it. His hair was long, tangled, and greasy. It hung down and you could see his eyes shining through like he was behind some vines. It was all black, no gray. So was his long shaggy beard. There was no color in his face, where his face showed. It was white, but not like a person. It was a kind of white that would make a person sick to see: tree-toad white, or fish-belly white. As for his clothes, they were just rags. He sat with one ankle resting on the other knee. The boot on that foot was broken and two of his toes stuck through. He moved them now and then as he talked. His hat was on the floor—an old black slouch hat with the top caved in, like a lid.

I stood looking at him and he sat there looking at me. His chair was tilted back just a little. I set the candle down and noticed the window was

up. He must have climbed in by the shed. He kept
looking me over. Finally he said:

"Nice clothes. You think you're pretty special
now, *don't* you?"

"Maybe I am, maybe I'm not," I said.

"Don't give me none of your lip," he said.
"You've put on great frills since I've been away.
You're educated, too, they say. You can read and
write. You think you're better than your father,
now, don't you? Just because he can't? Who told
you to mess with such foolishness, hey? Who said
you could?"

"The widow. She told me."

"They widow, hey? And who told her she
could stick her nose in someone else's business?"

"Nobody ever told her," I said.

"Well I'll teach her how to meddle. Look here,
you drop that school, you hear? I'll teach those
people to bring up a boy to think he's better than

his own father. Don't let me catch you fooling around at that school again. Your mother couldn't read or write before she died. None of her family could before *they* died. I can't, and here you're acting up like this. I'm not going to stand it. Say, let me hear you read."

I took up a book and started something about a war. After about half a minute, he knocked the book out of my hand.

"It's true," he said. "You can do it. I had my doubts. Look here, you stop putting on those frills acting like you're better than me. I won't have it."

He sat there mumbling and grumbling for a minute. Then he said:

"Aren't you fancy? A bed, bedclothes, a piece of carpet on the floor, and your own father has to sleep outside with the hogs. I've been in town two days and all I hear about is how you're rich now. I heard about it all the way down the river. That's why I came back. You get that money for me tomorrow. I want it."

"I don't have any money," I said.

"You're lying. Judge Thatcher's got it. You get it. I want it."

"I don't have any money. You can ask Judge Thatcher. He'll tell you the same."

"All right, I'll ask him. I'll make him talk, too. Say, how much do you have in your pockets? Give it to me."

"I only have about a dollar and I want that to——"

"It doesn't make a difference why you want it," he said. "Hand it over."

He took the money and bit down on the coins to check if they were real. Then he said he was going to town to have some fun and get into trouble. Finally he climbed out of the window. But then he stuck his head back in and had more bad words for me about my new life and how I was trying to be better than him. Just when I thought he was really gone, he stuck his head back in again and told me to stay away from school. He said he would be watching out for me there.

CHAPTER 3

Pap's Cabin

⌒

The next day Pap went to Judge Thatcher's office. He bullied the judge and tried to make him give up the money, but it didn't work. Then pap swore he'd get the money through the courts.

There was a new judge in town and he didn't know my pap. The new judge said the courts must not separate families if they could help it. He said he'd rather not take a child away from his father. So Judge Thatcher and the widow had to give up trying to keep pap away from me.

Pretty soon my pap went after Judge Thatcher

in the courts to make him give up that money. He chased after me, too, for not stopping school. He caught me a couple of times, but I went to school just the same. Most of the time I just dodged him or outran him. I hadn't liked school that much before, but now I liked it just to spite my pap.

He started hanging around the widow's place, too. Finally she told him that she would make trouble for him if he didn't stop. Well that made him mad, so one day he waited for me in secret and grabbed me when I wasn't looking. He took me upriver to an old log hut. The hut was so deep in the forest that you couldn't find it if you didn't know where it was.

He kept me with him all the time. I never had a chance to run off. We spent all day in that old cabin. At night he always locked the door and put the key under his head. He had a gun he'd stolen and we fished and hunted. That was how we lived. Every once in a while he locked me in and went down to the store to trade fish and game for supplies.

It was kind of lazy and jolly, lying around all day with no books or studying to do. Two months or more passed and my clothes were all rags and dirt again. I couldn't figure out how I had liked it so much at the widow's place, where you had to wash and eat off a plate, comb your hair, go to bed and get up at regular times, and always be bothering about a book. I didn't want to go back. On the other hand, I also didn't want to stay with pap.

I had tried to get out of the cabin many times, but I could never find a way. The windows were too small and the chimney too narrow for me to climb. I had searched the place a hundred times. Finally, one day I found an old rusty wood-saw and started sawing at a section of the big bottom log. I wanted to make a hole just big enough to crawl through. It was a long job, but I was getting toward the end of it when I heard pap's gun in the woods. I hid the signs of my work and pretty soon pap came in.

He wasn't in a good mood, which was normal. He had been in town and everything was going wrong in the courts. It was a long, slow process. His lawyer said he might lose the case and I would have to go back to the widow. Well I didn't want *that*. At one point, pap got so angry talking about it that he kicked an old barrel and hurt his foot. He hopped around, yelling and cursing for a long time. He was angrier than ever.

The old man made me go to the boat to fetch the things he had brought. Outside, I thought it all over and decided I would leave with the gun and some fishing lines. I would hide in the woods when I ran away. I wouldn't stay in one place, but just march right across the country, mostly at night. I could hunt and fish to stay alive. I would get so far away that neither the old man nor the widow would ever find me.

After supper, pap was in a very bad mood. I

guessed he would be asleep soon. Then I could steal the key, or saw myself out. He didn't fall asleep, though. He groaned and moaned and thrashed around this way and that for a long time. At last I got so sleepy that I couldn't keep my eyes open. Before I knew it, I was sound asleep.

All of a sudden there was an awful scream and I was up. Pap was looking wild. He was skipping around and yelling about snakes. He said they were crawling up his legs and then he would jump and scream. But I couldn't see any snakes. I've never seen a man look so wild in his eyes. He was seeing things and I thought he might be sick, or even crazy. Pretty soon he got tired and fell down. Then he rolled over and over very fast. He was kicking things, grabbing at the air with his hands, and screaming that there were devils all over him. Finally he got tired again and laid still for a while, moaning.

"Tramp-tramp-tramp. That's the dead," he

said. "Tramp-tramp-tramp. They're coming after me, but I won't go. They're here! Don't touch me! Your hands are cold—let go! Oh, leave a poor devil alone."

Then he crawled away, begging to be left alone. He wrapped himself in a blanket and started to cry.

By and by, he jumped up and ran after me. He chased me around the hut calling me the Angel of Death. Once, he caught me by the jacket between my shoulders. I thought I was a goner, but I slid out of the jacket as quick as lightning and saved myself. Soon he was all tired out again and dropped down with his back against the door.

He dozed off pretty soon. I climbed up on a chair as quietly as I could and got the gun. I made sure it was loaded and laid it across a barrel, pointing it toward pap. Then I sat and waited for him to move. And how slow and still the time did drag along.

CHAPTER 4

A Discovery

⌒

"Get up! What are you doing?"

It was after sunrise and I had been sound asleep. Pap was standing over me looking sour and sick. He said:

"What are you doing with this gun?"

I realized he didn't know anything about what he had been doing last night, so I said:

"Somebody tried to get in. I was waiting for him."

"Why didn't you wake me up?"

"I tried, but I couldn't. I couldn't budge you."

"Well, all right. Don't stand there all day. Go out and see if there's a fish on the line for breakfast."

He unlocked the door and I ran out to the riverbank. I noticed some tree branches and things floating downstream, so I knew the river had begun to rise. I walked along the bank and saw a canoe. A beauty, too, about thirteen or fourteen feet long. I jumped into the water head first, clothes on and all, and swam for it. At first I thought my pap would be glad to see the canoe. It would be worth ten dollars at least. But when I got to shore, pap wasn't in sight. Just then I had another idea. I decided to hide the canoe. Then, instead of hiding in the woods when I ran away, I could go down the river about fifty miles and camp in one place for good.

I was pretty close to the cabin by this time. I kept thinking I could hear the old man coming, but I was finally able to get the canoe hidden.

Then I saw pap down the path. He was aiming the gun at some birds in the distance. He hadn't seen anything.

While pap and I rested after breakfast, I tried to think of a way to keep him and the widow from trying to follow me. That would be better than just hoping I could get away before they noticed I was gone. I couldn't figure it out for a while, but by and by pap sat up to drink some water and said:

"The next time a man comes prowling around here you wake me up, you hear? That man was up to no good. The next time you better wake me up."

Then he lay down and fell asleep. What he said gave me the very idea I wanted. I could fix it now so nobody would ever think of following me.

At about noon we got up and walked along the bank. The river was rising pretty fast and lots of driftwood was going by. Pretty soon, along came part of a raft—nine logs tied together. We went out and pulled it ashore. Pap wanted to head right to town and sell the logs, so he locked me in the cabin, took our little boat, and started towing the raft. It must have been around half-past three. I didn't think he would come back that night. I waited until I thought he was far enough away, and then I went to work with my saw. I was out of the cabin before he was on the other side of the river.

I took all of our supplies to the canoe: the corn meal, side of bacon, all the coffee and sugar, and the ammunition. I took the bucket and gourd, a dipper, a tin cup, my old saw, two blankets, the skillet, and the coffee pot. I also took fish-lines, matches and a few other things—everything that was worth a cent. I cleaned out the place. I wanted an axe, but there was only one and I had a special plan for it. Finally I packed up the gun.

I covered up the tracks I had made and patched up the hole I had cut in the back of the cabin. I stood on the riverbank and looked out over the river. All safe.

Then I took the axe and smashed in the door. It was all part of my plan. I beat it and hacked at it a lot. Then I poured some old pig's blood all around and dragged a sack full of rocks along the ground toward the river. That left gruesome-looking tracks, as if a body had been dragged. I wished Tom Sawyer was there. I knew he would have been interested in this kind of business and thrown in some fancy touches.

Next I pulled out some of my hair. I made sure the axe was covered with the pig's blood and stuck those bits of hair to the axe. I threw the axe into the corner of the cabin. Then I thought of one more thing. I took the sack of corn meal, tore a small hole in it, and left a trail going in the other direction from my canoe. I carried the sack through the grass to a shallow lake. I dropped the stone that pap used to sharpen his knife there, too, as if it was left by accident. Then I tied up the hole in the sack of corn meal and brought it back to the canoe.

It was about dark now, so I moved the canoe down the river under some willows that hung over the bank and waited for the moon to rise. I ate a bit and laid down in the canoe to think up a plan. I said to myself, they'll follow the tracks to the shore and look in the river for me. Then they'll follow that trail of corn meal to the lake and search around there. They'll think a robber killed me and took all the things. They won't ever look for anything but my dead body. They'll soon get tired of that and then they won't look for me anymore. I decided to hide out on Jackson's Island. I knew the place pretty well and nobody ever went there. Then I could paddle to the town at night, slink around, and pick up things I wanted.

I was pretty tired and soon fell asleep. When I woke up, I didn't know where I was for a minute.

I sat up and looked around, a little scared. Then I remembered. The river looked miles and miles across. The moon was so bright that I could have counted all the logs that drifted along, black and still. Everything was dead quiet. It looked late. It even smelled late, if you know what I mean. I don't know any other words to describe it.

I yawned and stretched and was about to unhitch and start paddling when I heard a sound on the water. I listened and pretty soon I made it out. It was that dull, regular kind of sound that comes from oars moving in the water when it's a still night. I peeped out through the willow branches and there it was: a little boat away across the water. I couldn't tell how many people were in it. It kept coming. When it got closer, I saw there was only one man in it. I thought it might be pap, even though I wasn't expecting him. Soon he came so close I could have reached out and touched him. Sure enough, it was pap.

I didn't lose any time. In a minute I was moving the canoe quietly down the river. I got a few miles away, then moved to the middle of the river. Pretty soon I would be passing the ferry landing and people might see me if I got too close. I got out among the driftwood. Then I laid down in the bottom of the canoe so no one would see me and let it just float.

I laid there and had a good rest, looking away into the sky. There wasn't a cloud in it. The sky looks ever so deep when you lay down on your back in the moonlight. I'd never known that before. And how far a person can hear on the water! I heard people talking at the ferry landing. I heard what they said, too. Every word of it. One man said the days were getting longer now, the nights shorter. Another said that this wasn't one of the short ones and then they laughed. I heard one man say it was nearly three o'clock in the morning. After that, the talk got farther and farther away. I couldn't make out the words anymore, but I could hear the mumble and now and then a laugh, too. But it seemed a long way off.

After a while, I sat up. There was Jackson's Island, covered with trees and looking big, dark, and solid, like a steamboat without any lights.

It didn't take me long to get there. I paddled the canoe into a section of the bank that I knew about. I hid among the willow branches. When I was done, nobody could have seen the canoe from the outside.

I went and sat on a log at the head of the island. I looked out on the big river and the black driftwood. At the town a few miles away there were three or four lights twinkling. A very big lumber raft was about a mile upstream. It was coming downstream and had a lantern in the middle of it. I watched it come creeping down. When it was nearby, I heard a man say, "Stern oars, there! Move her to starboard!" I heard it just as clearly as if the man was at my side.

There was a little gray in the sky now, so I stepped into the woods and laid down for a nap before breakfast.

CHAPTER 5

A Mysterious Campfire

The next morning I was lazy and didn't want to get up to cook breakfast. I was dozing off again when I heard a deep *"boom!"* away up the river. I looked out through a hole in the leaves and saw a lot of smoke on the water. It was a long way up, near the ferry landing. And there was the ferryboat full of people. I knew what was going on now. *"Boom!"* I saw the white smoke come out of the ferryboat's side. They were firing a cannon over the water, trying to make my body float to the top.

The ferryboat was floating with the current and soon I could see who was aboard. Pap, Judge Thatcher, Jo Harper, Tom Sawyer, his old Aunt Polly, Sid, and plenty more were there. Everybody was talking about the murder.

Soon they floated past and went out of sight around the island. I could hear the booming now and then, further and further off. After about an hour, I didn't hear it anymore. I felt bad about lying to them like this, but I didn't know what else to do. I didn't want my pap to find me and I didn't want to go back to my old life with the widow.

I knew I was all right now. Nobody else would come looking for me. I got my things from the canoe and set up a nice camp in the thick woods. I made a kind of tent out of my blankets to put my things under so the rain couldn't get at them. I also caught a catfish. Toward sundown I started my campfire and had supper.

When it got dark, I sat by the fire feeling satisfied. But by and by it also got sort of lonesome. I sat on the bank and listened to the water swishing along and counted the stars and drift logs. Then I went to bed. There's no easier way to feel better when you're lonesome. You get over it soon.

It went on like this for three days and nights. Every day was the same. After that I went exploring around the island. It felt like it all belonged to me and I wanted to know all about it. I found plenty of strawberries and green summer grapes. Green raspberries and the blackberries were just beginning to come out. They would come in handy, I thought.

I almost caught a snake, too. I was running after it when, all of a sudden, I stepped right into the ashes of a campfire that was still smoking. Someone else was on my island!

My heart jumped up into my lungs. I didn't

wait to look around, but went sneaking back on my tiptoes as fast as I could. Every now and then I stopped and listened, but I was breathing so hard I couldn't hear anything else.

When I got back to camp, I wasn't feeling very brave. I told myself that this was no time to fool around. I gathered all my gear and put out my fire. I spread the ashes around to look like an old camp from last year and then I climbed up a tree.

I was up there for about two hours, but I didn't see or hear anything. There were a few times when my imagination made me think I heard and saw many things coming. I couldn't stay up there forever, so I finally climbed down. I stayed in the thick woods and kept on the lookout all the time. All I could eat were berries and leftovers from breakfast.

By nighttime I was pretty hungry. When it was good and dark, I moved the canoe out and paddled across the river. I went into the woods and cooked a supper. I had almost decided to stay there all night when I heard horses coming. Then I heard people's voices. I got everything back into the canoe as fast as I could and then crept through the woods to see what I could find out. I hadn't got far when I heard a man talking.

"We should camp here if we can find a place," he said. "The horses are tired."

I didn't wait, but shoved the canoe out and paddled away. I hid back on the island where I had been before and decided to sleep in the canoe.

I didn't sleep much. I couldn't. Every time I woke up I thought someone had caught me by the neck. Finally I said to myself, I can't live this way. I'm going to find out who's on this island with me. One way or another, I'll find out. Well, I felt better right away.

In the morning, I looked around some more and caught a glimpse of a fire away through the trees. I moved toward it, cautious and slow. Soon

I was close enough to see a man lying on the ground and covered with a blanket. He yawned, stretched, and took off the blanket.

It was Jim! I sure was glad to see him. I said:

"Hello Jim," and walked out.

He jumped up and stared at me with a scared look in his eyes. Then he fell to his knees and put his hands together and said:

"Don't hurt me! I never did any harm to a ghost. I always liked dead people and did all I could for them. You've got to get back in the river where you belong. Don't do anything to old Jim. I was always your friend."

Well it didn't take long to make him understand that I wasn't dead and I wasn't a ghost. I was ever so glad to see Jim. I wasn't lonesome now. I knew he wouldn't tell anyone where I was.

"How long have you been on the island?" I asked.

"I came here the night after you were

killed—or, the night people thought you were killed."

We went to where I had hidden the canoe. I fetched some food while he built a fire. When breakfast was ready, we laid on the grass and ate. Jim was starving. When we were both pretty much stuffed, was lay back and felt lazy. By and by Jim said:

"But, look here, who was killed in that cabin if it wasn't you?"

I told him the whole thing, about the pig's blood and the pretend tracks and everything, and he said it was smart. He said Tom Sawyer couldn't have thought up a better plan. Then I said:

"How did you get here, Jim?"

He looked pretty uneasy and didn't say anything for a minute. Then he said:

"Well, you see, it's this way. Old Miss Watson treats me pretty bad sometimes, but she always said that she wouldn't sell me down to New

Orleans. Then I noticed there was a slave trader coming around a lot recently and I began to get uneasy. Well, one night I crept to the door pretty late and I heard Miss Watson tell the widow that she was going to sell me down to New Orleans. She said she didn't want to, but she could get eight hundred dollars for me. It was so much money that she couldn't resist. The widow tried to talk her out of it, but I didn't wait to hear the rest. I ran away pretty fast, I tell you."

After Jim finished telling me his story, I showed him all the supplies I had with me and we ate a good dinner. It was his first good dinner since he'd run away. Then we found a good hiding place to set up camp.

CHAPTER 6

The House on the River

ᥴᔆ

The river kept on rising for ten or twelve days, until at last it was over the banks. The water was three or four feet deep on the island. During the day, we would paddle all over the island in the canoe. It was cool and shady in the deep woods, even if the sun was blazing.

One night, just before daylight, a whole house came floating down the river. It was two stories tall and tilted over. We paddled to it and climbed in an upstairs window. There was something laying on the floor in the far corner that looked like a man. So Jim said:

"Hello, you!"

But the figure didn't budge. So I hollered, and then Jim said:

"That man ain't asleep. He's dead. You hold still. I'll go and see."

He went in, looked at the man and said:

"It's a dead man. Yes, indeed. He's been shot in the back. It looks like he's been dead for two or three days. Come in, Huck, but don't look at his face. It's too scary."

I didn't look at him at all. Jim threw some old rags over him to make sure I wouldn't see the man's face, but he didn't need to do that. I didn't want to see him. We loaded the things we found there into the canoe and paddled home.

After breakfast I wanted to talk about the dead man and guess how he had been killed, but Jim didn't want to. He said it would bring bad luck and the dead man might come back to haunt us. I didn't say any more about it, but I wished I knew who shot the man and why they did it.

The next morning I said it was getting slow and dull. I wanted to do something new. I decided to go across the river and find out what was happening. Jim liked the idea, but he said I must go in the dark and be very careful. Then he thought about it and said that I should put on some of the clothes we had found in the house and dress up like a girl. That way no one would think it was really me.

I rowed across the river and talked to an old woman there. She saw through my disguise right away and I felt a little foolish about it. But she only knew that I was a boy, not Huck Finn. She must have thought I was a runaway. From her I learned that people did believe that I was dead, but she said they thought that Jim had killed me! She said Jim had run away the same night I had disappeared, so he must have done it.

Even worse, she said people were on their way to Jackson's Island to search it that very night. She was sure they would catch the murderer. Well right away I made up an excuse to leave and headed back to our camp. When I got there, Jim was asleep. I said:

"Get up, Jim! There's not a minute to lose. They're after us!"

He didn't ask any questions. In fact, he never even spoke. But the way he moved showed he was scared. In half an hour we had everything on our raft. I got in the canoe and looked around. I couldn't see anyone coming. Then we tied the canoe to the raft, got both of them out on the river, and started out. Neither of us said a single word.

CHAPTER 7

On the Wreck

❦

We floated along the river for a few days and then we had a big storm. The rain poured down in a solid sheet. When the lightning glared we could see a steamboat that had crashed on some rocks ahead of us. We were drifting right toward her.

"Let's land on her, Jim."

But Jim was dead against it at first. He said:

"I don't want to go fooling around on any wreck. We're doing all right and we should leave this alone. There's probably a watchman on the wreck, anyway."

"There's nothing left to watch on her, Jim. It looks like it's about to break up and wash off down the river any minute. Besides, we might find something in the captain's room. Steamboat captains are always rich. Do you think Tom Sawyer would let this go by? Never. He would call it an adventure."

Jim grumbled a little, but finally he gave in. He said we shouldn't talk much, if we got aboard. The lightning showed us the wreck again just in time. We rowed over to it and tied the raft and canoe to the side.

We climbed aboard in the dark. Soon we were in front of the captain's door, which was open. Down the hall we saw a light. In the same moment we heard voices!

Jim said he was feeling sick and told me to come along with him. I said all

right and was going to start for the raft, but just
then I heard a voice say:

"Oh, please don't, boys. I swear, I won't ever
tell."

Another voice said, pretty loudly:

"It's a lie, Turner. You've acted this way before.
You always want more than your share and you've
always gotten it, too, because you've sworn that if
you didn't then you would tell on us. But this time
you've joked about it once too often. You're the
meanest, most disloyal hound in this country."

By this time Jim was already gone for the raft. I
was curious. I said to myself, Tom Sawyer would-
n't back out now, so I won't either. I crept along
until I was in the room right next to the men.
Inside I saw a man tied up and lying on the floor.
Two men were standing over him.

The man on the floor said:

"Oh, please don't, Bill. I won't ever tell on
you."

The two men started walking to where I was. I moved as fast as I could, but there wasn't much room. They walked into the room where I was hiding. I was cornered. Now I was sorry that I had been so curious. Luckily, they didn't see me. Instead they talked about the man on the floor.

"He's said he'll tell on us, and he will. It won't make a difference if we let him go now. He'll turn against us."

"I think you're right, Bill. Here's my idea. We'll look around this ship and take whatever we can find. Then we'll leave him here and head for shore. This boat can't last more than two hours before it breaks up and washes off downriver. No one will ever find him."

As soon as they left the room, I took off. I was in a cold sweat. It was dark outside and I whispered, "Jim!" He was next to me and answered right away. I said:

"Quick, Jim, there's no time. There's a gang of

murderers on board. If we don't get rid of their boat so these fellows can't get away, they're going to kill someone. If we can find their boat, we'll have them trapped so the sheriff can come and get them. I'll look on this side. You look on the other side. Start looking where we tied up our raft, and—

"Oh, no! Raft? There is no raft. She broke loose. She's gone and we're stuck!"

CHAPTER 8

The Fate of the Wreck

I caught my breath and almost fainted. Stuck on a wreck with a gang like that! But there was no time to be scared. We *had* to find their boat for ourselves. We searched and searched and finally we found it. We were almost on board when the door opened. One of the men looked out. He was standing just a couple of feet ahead of me, but he didn't see me. He moved back in to talk to the other man and I got into the boat with Jim right behind me. I cut the rope with my knife and away we went!

We didn't touch an oar. We didn't speak. We

barely breathed. We went gliding silently away from the wreck. Soon we were so far away that the darkness covered her completely. We were safe and we knew it.

When we were far downstream, we saw the lantern show like a little spark at the door for a second. We knew that the rascals now knew they had missed their boat. They were beginning to understand that they were in just as much trouble as their partner.

I started to worry about those men. I said to Jim:

"I'll think up some kind of story so I can get somebody to go for that gang and get them off that wreck."

Soon after, we found our raft. We were mighty glad to be on it again. We piled all of the stuff from the gang's boat onto the raft and Jim floated ahead with it a little ways. He lit a lantern so I could find him again later.

I took the boat and rowed to the shore. When I got there I found a watchman asleep next to a ferryboat. I told him about the gang on the wreck, but it was too late. After he left and I found Jim again, we saw the wreck itself, dim and dusky, sliding along down the river! A cold shiver went through me. The wreck was very deep in the water and I couldn't see anyone on board.

Before dawn, Jim and I hid the raft and the boat. Then we laid down and slept like dead people.

When we got up, we went through the stuff the gang had stolen. We found a lot of clothes, books, and other things. We had never been so rich in our lives. We spent the afternoon talking and I read from the books. I told Jim about what had happened inside the wreck and said these things were adventures. He said he didn't want any more of those.

I read to him about kings and dukes and earls.

The book described how they dressed and talked, calling each other your majesty, your grace, your lordship, and so on, instead of mister. Some of them even spoke French.

We guessed that it would take us three nights to get to Cairo, which was at the bottom of Illinois where the Ohio River comes in. We could sell the raft and take a steamboat into Ohio. From there we could get into the free States, where we would be out of trouble. Jim missed his children terribly and talked about getting someone to fetch them for him once he was in the free states. I knew there would be big trouble for each of us if we were caught before we could get there. Jim would be punished for running away, and I could get in trouble for helping him.

On the second night we got lost and separated in some fog. I was in the canoe and Jim was on the raft. It took us a long time to find each other again. When we did, we found we had drifted right past Cairo. We had no choice but to take the canoe back.

We slept all day among the cottonwood thicket so we could paddle back at night. When we went back to the raft after dark, the canoe was gone! We'd had a lot of bad luck by then and were mighty upset about it.

We didn't say a word for a good while. There wasn't anything to say. We decided to go along down the river on the raft until we found a chance to buy a canoe. Then we would try to paddle back. We didn't want to borrow one, the way pap would, for that might set people after us.

So we shoved out after dark on the raft. Then more bad luck hit us. The night got gray and thick, which is the next meanest thing to fog. You can't tell the shape of the river and you can't see far at all. It got to be very late and still. Just then, along came a steamboat up the river. We lit the lantern and judged she would see it.

We could hear her pounding along, but we didn't see her good till she was close. She aimed right for us. They often do that and try to see how close they can come without touching. Then the pilot sticks his head out and laughs and thinks he's mighty smart. Well here she comes, and she didn't seem to be veering off a bit. She was a big one and she was coming in a hurry, too, looking like a black cloud with rows of glow-worms around it. There was a yell at us, a jingling of bells to stop the engines, and a lot of cursing and whistling of steam. As Jim went overboard on one side and I fell off the other, she came smashing straight through the raft!

I dived—and I aimed to find the bottom, too. A thirty-foot wheel had to pass over me and I wanted it to have plenty of room. I could always stay under water for a minute. This time I reckon I stayed under a minute and a half. Then I bounced for the top in a hurry, for I was nearly busting. I popped out to my armpits, blew the water out of my nose, and puffed a bit. Of course there was a booming current, and of course that boat started her engines again ten seconds after she stopped them. They never cared much for people on rafts. Now she was churning along up the river. She was out of sight in the thick weather, although I could hear her.

I called out for Jim about a dozen times, but I didn't get any answer. Finally I grabbed a plank that touched me while I was treading water and struck out for shore, shoving it ahead of me.

It took a long time, but I finally made a safe landing. I couldn't see far and went poking along over rough ground for long time. Then I found a big old-fashioned log-house. I was going to pass it by, but a lot of dogs jumped out and started howling and barking at me.

After about a minute, somebody yelled out of the window and asked me for my name.

"George Jackson, sir," I said. "I'm only a boy."

"Look here, if you're telling the truth you needn't be afraid. Nobody will hurt you. But don't try to budge. Stand right where you are. Go get Bob and Tom, some of you. Is there anybody with you, George Jackson?"

"No, sir. Nobody."

"Now, George Jackson, do you know the Shepherdsons?"

"No, sir. I never heard of them."

"Well, that may be so and it may not. Step forward, George Jackson. And mind, don't you hurry. Come mighty slow. Push the door open yourself—just enough to squeeze in, do you hear?"

I didn't hurry. I couldn't if I'd wanted to. I heard them unlocking and unbarring and unbolting the door. I pushed it a little and looked inside.

The candle was on the floor. There were all standing there looking at me. I looked back at them. The three big men staring at me made me wince, I tell you. The oldest of them was gray and about sixty. The other two were thirty or older. All of them were fine and handsome. Behind them was a sweet old gray-headed lady. Behind her were two young women.

The old gentleman locked, barred, and bolted the door as soon as I was in. He told the young men to come in. They took a good look at me and said:

"Why, *he* ain't a Shepherdson. No, there ain't any Shepherdson about him."

Then the old man said he hoped I wouldn't mind being searched for weapons. He didn't mean any harm by it. It was only to make sure. He told me to make myself easy and at home. He said I should tell them all about myself, but the old lady said:

"Why, bless you, Saul, the poor thing's as wet as can be. Don't you reckon he's hungry?"

"True for you, Rachel, I forgot."

So the old lady said:

"Betsy, get him something to eat as quick as you can, poor thing. Buck, go upstairs and find some clothes to give him."

Buck looked about as old as me—thirteen or fourteen or along there, though he was a little bigger than me.

I made up a story and told them I had fallen off a steamboat and I was an orphan. They said I could have a home there as long as I wanted it. Then it was almost daylight and everybody went to bed. When I woke up in the morning, drat it all, I had forgotten what I told them my name was. I laid there for about an hour trying to think and when Buck woke up I asked if he could spell.

"I bet you can't spell my name," I said.

"G-e-o-r-g-e J-a-x-o-n—there now," he said.

"Well," I said, "you did it, but I didn't think you could."

I made sure to remember it, in case anybody would ask *me* how to spell my name. I learned that this family was named Grangerford.

There was Colonel Grangerford, who was very tall and very slim. He had the blackest kind of eyes, sunk so deep back that they seemed like they were looking out of caverns at you. His hair was black and straight and hung to his shoulders.

He carried a wooden cane with a silver head to it. He was as kind as he could be. You could feel that. Sometimes he smiled and it was good to see.

But when he looked angry, you wanted to climb a tree first and find out what the matter was afterward. He didn't ever have to tell anybody to mind their manners. Everybody was always good-mannered around him.

Bob was the oldest son and Tom next. They were both tall, beautiful men with very broad shoulders, brown faces, long black hair, and black eyes. They dressed in white linen from head to foot, like the old Colonel, and wore broad Panama hats.

Then there was Miss Charlotte. She was twenty-five, tall, and proud. She was beautiful and kind, but she could get angry just like her father. Her sister, Miss Sophia, was also beautiful, but it was a different kind. She was gentle and sweet like a dove. She was only twenty.

There was another family around there whose name was Shepherdson. They were as rich and grand as the Grangerfords. From Buck I learned that the two families had been fighting with each other for many years. No one remembered how it all started, but whenever a Shepherdson and a Grangerford were near, they started shooting at each other.

CHAPTER 9

The Families Feud

⌒

The next Sunday we all went to church. After dinner that night, Miss Sophia asked me to get her Bible from the church because she had forgotten it there. I went to the church and found her Bible. It seemed strange to me that she would be so nervous about it. When I shook the book, a note fell out with "half-past two" written on it.

When I got home, Miss Sophia took me to her room and looked in the Bible. When she found and read the note, she asked if I had read it. I lied and told her I couldn't read. Then she hugged me and told me to go out and play.

Outside, one of the slaves was following me. When I asked him why, he said he had something important to show me. I followed him down to the swamp, far from the house. He pointed to an area in the distance, told me to look in there, and then left.

I found a little open patch as big as a bedroom hung all around with vines. There was a man laying there asleep. It was old Jim!

I woke him up. He was so happy to see me that he nearly cried. He said he had followed me in the water the night we were separated, but he couldn't call out for me because he was afraid someone would have heard him and caught him.

"Why didn't you come and get me sooner, Jim?"

"Well, I've been busy gathering supplies and fixing the raft—"

"*What* raft, Jim?"

"Our old raft."

"You mean it wasn't smashed to pieces?"

"No, she was torn up a good, but I was able to fix her up just fine. When I saw that you were safe in the old house, I made friends with some of their slaves, and they kept me hidden here."

I told Jim to stay put and then headed back up to the house.

I don't want to talk much about the next day. I reckon I'll cut it pretty short. I woke up early, and noticed how still it was. There didn't seem to be anybody stirring, which was unusual. Buck was gone and the house was empty. I went outside and asked one of the slaves, who told me that Miss Sophia had run away with one of the Shepherdsons. They were in love! Both families were off in a battle with each other now.

I ran toward the river and soon heard guns. I climbed up a tree and watched the battle. It was horrible. The two families were fighting fiercely and shooting at each other. I found Buck and he told me about Miss Sophia running away with young Harney Shepherdson. Buck said they'd got across the river safely. I was glad of that, but Buck was angry that he had never shot Harney. I had never heard anything like it.

All of a sudden, *bang! bang! bang!* went three or four guns. Buck and the boys with him jumped for the river. Both of them seemed to be hurt. As they swam down the current, some men ran along the bank shooting at them. It made me so sick that I almost fell out of the tree. I won't tell *all* that happened next. It would make me sick again if I was to do that. I wished I had never come ashore that night to see such things. I won't ever forget them.

I stayed in the tree until it began to get dark. I was afraid to come down. Sometimes I heard guns away off in the woods. Twice I saw little gangs of men gallop past with guns, so I reckoned the trouble was still going on. I was mighty down-hearted. I made up my mind I wouldn't ever go near that house again. I thought I was to blame, somehow. I judged that that piece of paper meant that Miss Sophia was to meet Harney somewhere at half-past two and run off. I should have told her father about that paper and the curious way she acted. Then maybe this awful mess wouldn't have happened.

When I got down out of the tree I crept along down the riverbank. I cried a little for Buck, for he had been mighty good to me. It was dark now. I never went near the house, but struck through the woods and made for the swamp. My souls, but I was scared! I raised a yell. A voice nearby said:

"Is that you?"

It was Jim's voice—nothing ever sounded so good before. I ran along the bank and got aboard our raft. Jim was so glad to see me that he grabbed me and hugged me. Then he said:

"Bless you, child, I was sure you were dead again. The slaves came earlier and they thought you had been shot. I'm so glad to get you back again."

"All right, that's mighty good. They won't find me. They'll think I've been killed and floated down the river. Don't lose time, Jim. Just shove off for the big water as fast as you can."

I was powerfully glad to get away from the fighting and so was Jim to get away from the swamp. We said there was no home like a raft, after all. Other places do seem so cramped up and smothery, but a raft doesn't. You feel mighty free and easy and comfortable on a raft.

CHAPTER 10

A King and a Duke

Two or three days and nights went by, quiet, smooth, and lovely. It was a huge river—sometimes a mile and a half wide. We traveled at night and hid the raft just before daylight. Then we would have a swim and watch the daylight come.

As soon as it was night, we took the raft out to the middle of the river and let her float wherever the current wanted. Then we relaxed, dangled our legs in the water, and talked about all kinds of things. We were always naked, day and night. At least whenever the mosquitoes would let us be.

The new clothes Buck's folks gave me were too good to be comfortable. And besides, I didn't like clothes much.

Sometimes we had that whole river to ourselves for the longest time. Sometimes you could see a spark or two—candles or lanterns—on a raft or in a cabin near the shore. Once in a while you could hear a fiddle or a song coming over from somewhere. It's lovely to live on a raft. The sky was speckled with stars. We would lie on our backs and just look up at them.

One morning I paddled upriver a bit to see if I could get some berries. Just as I was passing a place where a path crossed the creek, a couple of men came running up the path as fast as they could. I thought I was a goner for sure. Whenever anybody was after anyone else, I always thought it was *me,* or maybe Jim. I was about to paddle away, but they were pretty close by then and they called out and begged me to save their lives. They said they hadn't been doing anything wrong, but they were being chased. There were men and dogs coming.

They got aboard and in a few minutes we heard the dogs and the men away off, shouting. I paddled in among the trees and hid us from them.

One of these fellows was about seventy. He had a bald head and very gray whiskers. He was wearing an old beaten-up slouch hat, a greasy blue shirt, and ragged old blue jeans stuffed into his boot-tops. The other fellow was about thirty and dressed the same. Both of the men had big, fat, ratty-looking carpet-bags.

After breakfast we talked. The first thing that came out was that these chaps didn't know one another.

"What got you into trouble?" the bald-headed one asked.

"Well, I'd been selling an article to take the

yellow off the teeth. And it does take it off, too. It just takes the enamel along with it. But I stayed about one night longer than I ought to. I was just about to get away when I ran across you on the trail. You told me they were coming and begged me to help you to get away. So I told you I was expecting trouble myself and would scatter out *with* you. That's the whole yarn. What's yours?"

"Well," said the bald-headed man, "I'd been running a little religious meeting there for about a week, talking to the folks about how they should behave. I was taking in as much as five or six dollars a night—ten cents a head—when somehow a report got around last night that I had been behaving badly on the sly. This morning I heard the people were gathering. If they got me they said they'd tar and feather me and ride me on a rail."

"Old man," said the young one, "I reckon we

might double-team it together. What do you think?"

"I could do that. What's your line of work, mainly?"

"I'm a printer by trade, but I usually sell some medicines or work as a theater-actor. Oh, I can do lots of things—anything that comes in handy."

"I've done some doctoring in my time, too. I can tell a fortune pretty good when I've got somebody along to find out the facts for me. Preaching's my line, too."

Nobody said anything for a while. Then the young man sighed and said:

"Alas!"

"What are you alas-ing about?" asked the bald-headed man.

"To think I should be leading such a life. And to be forced into such company..." He began to wipe the corner of his eye with a rag.

"Ain't the company good enough for you?" says the baldhead.

"Yes, it *is* good enough for me. It's as good as I deserve. I don't blame *you,* gentlemen—far from it. I don't blame anybody. I deserve it all. I brought myself down. Yes, I did it myself."

"Brought you down from where?"

"Ah, you would not believe me. The secret of my birth—"

"The secret of your birth! Do you mean to say—"

"Gentlemen," said the young man very seriously, "I will reveal it to you, for I feel I may have confidence in you. By rights I am a duke! I am the rightful Duke of Bridgewater!"

He started to cry about how he was so poor now. We tried to make him feel better, but he said he couldn't be comforted. He said we ought to bow when we spoke to him and say "your grace," "my lord," or "your lordship." He said he wouldn't mind it if we called him "Bridgewater," which was his title. He also told us that one of us ought to wait on him at dinner and do any little thing for him that he wanted done.

Well that was easy enough. We did it, and we could see it made him happier. But the old man got pretty silent and didn't look comfortable. He seemed to have something on his mind. Then, in the afternoon, he said:

"Look here, Bilgewater. I feel sorry for you, but you ain't the only person with troubles like that."

"Alas!"

"No, you ain't the only person with a secret." And then *he* began to cry.

"Bilgewater, you see before you, in blue jeans and misery, the wandering, exiled, trampled-on, and suffering, rightful King of France!"

It didn't take me long to make up my mind that these liars weren't kings nor dukes at all, but just low-down frauds. I never said a thing to let on that I knew the truth. I had no objections if they wanted us to call them kings and dukes, as long as it would keep everything peaceful on the raft. If I learned anything from pap, it was that the best way to get along with his kind of people is to let them have their own way.

They asked us a lot of questions about why we would hide the raft during the daytime and who we were running from, so I made up a story for them. I told them that most of my family was gone and that Jim and I had been living on the raft with my pa and my little brother, but that they had fallen off the raft when we were hit by a steamboat.

That night it started to rain. The duke and the king argued a bit over who would sleep in beds.

Mine was a bit better than Jim's and both were under a little wigwam that Jim had made out of some blankets. While the two liars slept in our beds, Jim and I stayed up and kept watch during the storm.

CHAPTER 11

The Camp Meeting

The next day, the king and the duke had an idea about how they might be able to make some money in the next little town. Jim stayed on the raft while I went with the king and the duke.

When we got to the town, the streets were empty and perfectly still. The duke found a printing-office and said he could do some work there. The king learned of a camp meeting, so he took me with him to it.

There were almost a thousand people at the meeting, which was inside a large shed. Everyone sat on benches and listened to people talking about their lives and religion. The women wore sun-bonnets and some of the young men were barefoot. The old women were knitting and the young folks were flirting on the sly.

The preacher had everyone excited. They were all singing and shouting. I thought it was crazy and wild. Well before I knew it, the king started yelling and talking like the preacher. The king even climbed on stage and started telling the people he had been a pirate for thirty years out in the Indian Ocean. He said he had come here looking for a new crew. But after hearing these people, he told the crowd, he was a changed man. He said he wanted to go back to the Indian Ocean to talk to the other pirates and get them to change their lives.

And then he burst into tears. Everyone else began to cry, too. Then somebody yelled, "Take up a collection for him, take up a collection!" So the king went all through the crowd with his hat. By the time we got back to the raft, he had collected eighty-seven dollars and seventy-five cents!

The next morning, the king and the duke practiced their lines for a play called *Romeo and Juliet*. It was pretty rough to hear. Then they got out a couple of long swords that the duke made out of some branches and practiced a swordfight. They also made up some more things to do on stage. Finally they decided that they had a whole show. They tried the play in town that night and it was awful. Hardly anyone showed up.

Well the duke had learned of a circus that was in the next town. He had made up some new posters for the show that he and the king wanted to do. The poster said it would be "grand," and that "Ladies and children would not be admitted."

"If that doesn't get them to come to the show, I don't know what will," the duke said.

All the next day
the king and the duke
worked hard. They set up a stage
with curtains and a row of candles for lights.
They also discussed some new ideas for the night's
show. That night the place was packed full of men.
Each had paid fifty cents to get in. The duke's
poster had worked on them.

The duke came out on stage and talked about
the play. He told the men over and over again
how great it was. When he'd finally raised everyone's hopes up high enough, he rolled up the
curtain. Then the king came out crawling on his
hands and knees. His whole body was painted different colors. He was as colorful as a rainbow. It
was wild, but it was also awfully funny. The audience almost died laughing. When the king finished prancing around on stage, they roared and
clapped until he came back and did it over again.
After that they made him do it another time. It

would have made a cow laugh to see that old man.

Then the duke closed the curtains and said that was the end of the show. Twenty people called out:

"What, is it over? Is that *all*?"

The duke said yes. Then there was a fine time. Everybody yelled and stood up. They were mad and were going to attack the stage and the two actors. But just then a big man shouted:

"Hold on! Just a word, gentlemen. They got us all right, but we don't want to be the laughing stock of this whole town. We should leave quietly and talk this show up. We could sell the *rest* of the town on it! Then we'll all be in the same boat. Ain't that smart?"

The next day the place was full again. The king and the duke put on the same show for the new men. Then on the third night the house was crammed again. All of the people who were at the shows the first two nights had come back. I saw that every man had bulging pockets. Some held something bundled up under their coats. I smelled rotten eggs and cabbages. When the place couldn't hold any more people, the duke started around for the stage door and I followed him. The minute we turned the corner and were in the dark, he said:

"Walk fast now till you get away from the houses. Then run for the raft like the devil was after you!"

We got to the raft pretty quickly and were soon all out on the river again. The duke said he knew the audience would try to fool us by coming back to throw rotten food at us. They wanted revenge for being fooled the other two nights.

The king and the duke weren't upset, though. They took in four hundred and sixty-five dollars in those three nights! I never saw money hauled in by the wagon-load like that before.

CHAPTER 12

Harvey and William Wilks

ᴄᴏ

A few days later the king and the duke wanted to try that game again. We hid the raft and Jim and the duke stayed with it. Then the king and I took a steamboat across the river. While we were on it, one of the other passengers started talking to the king. He told us about a family nearby that was expecting some visitors soon.

The young man told us that two brothers named Peter and George Wilks had died recently, first George, then Peter. Their other brothers, Harvey and William, were coming because Peter had sent for them before he died. The young man then told us that William couldn't hear or speak.

The young man said Peter had left a letter for Harvey, which said where he had hidden his money and how he wanted his property divided up after he was dead. He wanted to make sure that George's daughters would be all right.

"Why hasn't Harvey arrived yet? Where does he live?" the king asked.

"Oh, he lives in England—Sheffield. He preaches there. Harvey has never been in this country. He hasn't had too much time, and besides, he might not have even received the letter at all, you know."

"Poor things!" the king said. "For those girls to be left alone in the cold world so."

Well, the king went on asking questions until he had almost emptied that young fellow. He asked about everybody and everything in that town. He learned all about the Wilkses. He found out that Peter was a tanner, that George was a carpenter, that Harvey was a minister, and so on, and so on.

"Was Peter Wilks well off?"

"Oh, yes, pretty well off," said the young man. "He had houses and land, and it's reckoned he left three or four thousand in cash hidden somewhere."

"When did you say he died?"

"I didn't say, but it was last night."

"Funeral tomorrow, likely?"

"Yes, about the middle of the day."

"Well, it's all terribly sad, but we've all got to go at one time or another. So what we want to do is to be prepared. Then we're all right."

"Yes, sir, it's the best way. Ma used to always say that."

When we landed at the other side and everyone else was gone, the king said:

"Now hustle back and fetch the duke up here. And bring the carpet-bags. Hurry now!"

I knew what he was up to, but I never said anything, of course. When I came back with the duke, the king told him everything. He repeated the information just like the young fellow had said it—every last word of it. And all the time he tried to talk like an Englishman. He did it pretty well. Then he said:

"How are you on pretending that you can't hear or speak, Bilgewater?"

The duke said he had acted that way before on stage.

When we got to the village, about two dozen men saw us coming and ran down to meet us.

"Can any of you gentlemen tell me where Mr. Peter Wilks lives?" the king asked, in his funny accent.

The men looked at one another and nodded

their heads. Then one of them said in a kind of soft and gentle voice:

"I'm sorry, sir, but the best we can do is to tell you where he *did* live yesterday evening."

The king started to cry and said:

"Alas, alas, our poor brother! Gone, and we never got to see him. Oh, it's too, too hard!"

Then he turned around, blubbering, and made some signs to the duke with his hands. And then the duke started crying!

The men gathered around and tried to comfort them. They said all sorts of kind things to them and carried their carpet-bags up the hill for them. They let the king and the duke lean on them and cry while they told the king all about his brother's last moments. Then the king used his hands to tell the duke everything he had heard. I had never seen anything like them in my life.

CHAPTER 13

The Duke's Plan

༄

The news was all over town in minutes and pretty soon we were in the middle of a crowd. The windows and front yards were full. Every so often somebody would say over a fence:

"Is it *them*?"

And somebody walking along with us would answer:

"You bet it is."

When we got to the house, the street in front was packed with people. There were three girls standing at the door. Luckily, we knew who everyone was from the story the young man had told us the other day. Mary Jane was the oldest. She had red hair and she was very beautiful. Her face and eyes were all lit up. She was so happy her uncles had come. The king spread his arms and Mary Jane jumped for them. Another daughter, who had a hard time speaking, hugged the duke. The third daughter just stood by and watched.

Then the king and the duke saw the coffin, which was propped up on two chairs. They walked over to it very seriously and covered their eyes as if they were upset. Everybody gave them room and all the talk and noise stopped. The two men stood in front of the coffin for a few seconds and then burst out crying. Then they kneeled next to the coffin and pretended to pray over it. That worked on the crowd so well. You've never seen anything like it. Everybody broke down crying.

By and by, the king stood and gave a speech. It

was all full of tears and nonsense about how hard it was for him and his poor brother to lose Peter. He talked about how upset he was to miss seeing him alive after the long journey from England. He talked about almost everybody in town, mentioning as many people by name as the young man the other day had told us. The king also mentioned all sorts of little things that had happened at one time or another around town, or to George's or Peter's family. He always made it sound as if Peter had written to him about all of these things, but that was a lie. He had heard every little detail from that young man on the steamboat.

Then Mary Jane fetched the letter that her uncle had left behind. The king read it out loud and cried over it. It explained how Peter wanted his fortune divided up among the girls and his brothers. It also described where six thousand dollars was hidden in the cellar. The two frauds took me downstairs with them. When we found the bag, they spilled the money out on the floor.

"I've got an idea," the duke said. "Let's go upstairs, count out the money, and then give it to the girls!"

"Why, that's the best idea you've had. They've got to believe we're their uncles if we give them the money," the king said.

Back upstairs, the king made another slobbering speech about old Peter Wilks and then gave the bag full of money to Mary Jane. She hugged him and the other two daughters went to hug and kiss the duke.

Well pretty soon the king was talking about the dead man again. The duke had to pretend he couldn't hear or speak, but the king didn't have any problems with talking. He went on and on. I thought it was terrible, even though most of the people seemed to believe him.

Just then there was a loud noise in the crowd and someone spoke up:

"Why, Doctor Robinson! Haven't you heard? That man is Harvey Wilks," said someone.

The king smiled and tried to shake hands with the doctor.

"Keep your hands off me!" the doctor said. "You think you talk with an English accent? That's the worst imitation I've ever heard. You aren't Peter Wilks' brother. You're a fraud!"

Well the crowd became very upset at that. The king was able to convince almost everybody that he really *was* Harvey Wilks. When Mary Jane said *she* believed him, that seemed to settle it for everybody but old Doctor Robinson.

That night we had a big dinner with the daughters. Then they set the king, the duke, and me up with a room each. I spent some time talking with each daughter. It wasn't easy, let me tell you. I was trying to imitate the king's English accent. I thought they would see through me right away, but they didn't. I started to see that these girls were kind and didn't deserve to have their money stolen by those two old frauds. I felt so mean and low down that I made up my mind to get that money away from the king and the duke.

I laid in bed that night trying to think up a way to fool those two men. I decided to steal the money from them and hide it somewhere. Then I could leave a note for Mary Jane telling her where I hid it. That way she could get the money after we left.

I started to search the king's room, but I had to hide when I heard the two men coming up the stairs. The came in and talked about their plans. It was awful to hear. They wanted to steal the six thousand dollars. I knew that much already. But they also wanted to sell the house and all of the property that Peter Wilks owned. They wanted to leave the girls with nothing!

The duke grumbled that he didn't want to rob a lot of orphans of *everything* they had.

"How you talk," said the king. "We'll only be robbing them of this cash. Whoever buys the properties will have to give them all back to the girls as soon as they find out that we aren't really the Wilks brothers. It's the law. They aren't going to suffer at all."

Well, the king talked and talked until the duke gave in. After that they hid the bag of money and went back downstairs to say good night to everyone.

I had the bag before they were halfway down the stairs. Then I went back to my room. I guessed they wouldn't miss the money for a little while, but I knew they would come looking for it as soon as they found it gone. I wanted to hide it as soon as I could.

I waited until I was sure everyone was asleep. Then I crept downstairs with the money. I saw

the coffin in the parlor. The funeral was set for the next day. I went in and looked around. The only place I could see to hide the money was in the coffin. I tucked the bag in under the lid, just below where the man's hands were crossed. It sent shivers down his spine. His hands were so cold.

Well the next day was the funeral. It sure was strange to see the coffin being buried. I was the only one who knew that there was six thousand dollars hidden in it!

That night the king told the girls that he and William had to hurry back to England. He wanted the girls to settle their estate as soon as possible. He said that they should have an auction for the house and all the properties. He even said that he and William would take the girls back to England! It pleased the girls so much to hear that. They agreed right away and told the king to sell off everything as quickly as he wanted.

CHAPTER 14

Huck's Confession

The king and the duke woke me up early the next morning. I could tell from their faces that there was trouble.

"Were you in my room last night or the night before?" the king asked.

"No, your majesty," I said.

"Have you seen anybody else go in there?" the duke asked.

I pretended to think for a while and then I told them I'd seen some of the slaves go into the king's room a few times.

Both of them gave a little jump and looked like they had never expected that. Then their expressions changed and they looked like they *had* expected the slaves to take the money.

"Great guns, *this* is a go!" the king said.

Both of them looked pretty sick and silly. They stood there thinking and scratching their heads for a minute. Then the duke burst into a kind of raspy little chuckle. They talked about how smart those slaves were. I asked if anything was wrong. Well they got very mad at me for asking that and for not telling them I'd seen the slaves going into the king's room. The slaves had left the house the day before when news had spread that the men were going to auction off all the property.

I knew the two men didn't want to tell me the money was gone. They didn't think I knew they had the money in the first place! They didn't think I knew any of their plans to rob the girls.

The next day I saw Mary Jane crying. When I went to talk to her, she told me that she was upset about leaving her home. She said she was excited to be going to England soon, but it made her sad to leave her home. Well, seeing her cry like that and seeing that she believed those two frauds were really her uncles, I just couldn't keep lying to her.

"I've got to tell the truth," I said. "You'll want to brace up, Miss Mary, because it's a bad kind. It's going to be hard to take, but there's no help for it. These uncles of yours aren't uncles at all. They're a couple of frauds—regular dead-beats."

It surprised her, of course, but I was over the worst of it now so I went right along and told her every last detail. I described everything that had happened from the time we met that young fool on the steamboat clear through to when she hugged and kissed the king the day she met him.

Then, with her face red like sunset, she stood and said:

"The brute! Come, don't waste a minute— not a *second*. We'll have them tarred and feathered and flung in the river!"

"Well," I said, "it's a rough gang, those two frauds. And I've got to travel with them a while longer, whether I want to or not. I'd rather not tell you why. If you were to tell on them, this town would get me out of their claws. I'd be all right, but there'd be another person that you don't know about who'd be in big trouble. Well, we've got to save *him*, don't we? Of course. Well, then, we can't tell on them yet."

Talking to her, I had an idea of how I could lose those two frauds. I asked Mary Jane to stay at her friend's house, which was a few miles away, while I worked on my plan. Then she was to come back here. If I wasn't back by eleven o'clock, she was to tell everyone the truth about the king and the duke.

After Mary Jane left, I went outside to where the auction was being held in the public square. It was late in the afternoon and it took a long time to sell everything. The king kept giving speeches and interrupting the auctioneer while the duke pretended to talk with sign language. Eventually they sold everything. Just as the auction was ending, a crowd came up from the steamboat dock. They were yelling, laughing, and carrying-on.

"Here's another set of heirs to old Peter Wilks' fortune!" they yelled. "Two more brothers!"

The crowd was walking with an older gentleman and a nice looking younger one. My souls, how the people yelled and laughed. I didn't see any joke about it. I thought surely the king and the duke would get upset. But no, they just looked at the newcomers. The king had a sad look on his face, as if it made him sick to think there could be such frauds in the world. The nice old gentleman looked confused. When he spoke, I knew right away that he had a real English accent. It was nothing like the king's fake accent.

There were a lot of arguments then. The newcomers said they were the real Harvey and William Wilks. They had been held up in their journey here and now they had to prove that *they* were telling the truth. The old doctor said he knew that the king and the duke were lying. He demanded that the six thousand dollars be returned. The king told him that the money was stolen by the slaves, who had since left town.

At first the town seemed divided between those who believed the king and the duke really were the Wilks brothers and those who believed in the newcomers. But as they listened to the real brothers, more people started to realize who was telling the truth and who was lying. The king put on a good show, though. He answered every question so well that it was hard to prove he was lying.

Finally the old gentleman asked the king to

describe a tattoo that was on the dead man's chest. The king said it was a tiny blue arrow. The older gentleman said it was the man's initials: PW. The doctor who had examined the body said he hadn't seen *any* tattoos. So everyone decided to dig up the grave and have a look at the body. That would decide once and for all who was telling the truth.

I *was* scared now, I tell you. But there was no getting away. They held on to us and marched us to the graveyard. A lot of people started digging. Soon it got dark. The rain started, the wind swished along, the lightning came, and the thunder boomed. But the people took no notice of it. Everyone was watching the grave.

At last they had the coffin out and began to open the lid. Then someone yelled:

"There's a bag of gold in here!"

The man who was holding on to my wrist let go and moved closer to the coffin along with everyone else. Well I started running as fast as I could! I ran back through the town in the rain. I couldn't see except for when the lightning flashed. I ran and ran. Finally I saw the river where Jim and the raft were hidden.

When I jumped aboard I said, "Jim, get up! We have to leave now!"

Jim was happy to see me and we were both happy to be rid of the king and the duke. In a few seconds we were moving down the river, but I could hear something familiar. I listened and listened and when the lightning flashed again, there they were! It was the king and the duke. They were in a canoe and rowing toward us as fast as they could.

It was all I could do to keep from crying.

They were mad at me for running away, but as they talked about how they escaped they agreed that I had done the right thing. It turned out that they had also run when the crowd moved in to see the bag of gold in the coffin. They were mad to have lost that money and couldn't figure out how it had all gotten into the coffin. Then they accused one another of trying to steal it. When they finally went to sleep that night, I stayed up and told Jim everything that had happened.

CHAPTER 15

Jim Vanishes

We didn't stop at a town again for days and days. We just kept on floating right down the river. Once the frauds reckoned they were out of danger, they started to work the villages again. They tried all sorts of tricks and games to make money, but none of them seemed to work. At last they were dead broke. They laid around on the raft, thinking and thinking. They were awfully sad and desperate.

After awhile they started talking together in private. This made Jim and me uneasy. We didn't like the look of things. We knew the old frauds were planning some kind of trouble. We decided to give them the cold shake at the first opportunity, then clear out and leave them behind.

At the next town, the king went ahead to look around. The duke and I followed a few hours later. We found the king getting in trouble and carrying-on. While he and the duke argued, I escaped. I ran back to the raft and called out to Jim, but there was no answer. He was gone! I searched and searched, but he was nowhere in sight. Finally I sat down and cried. I couldn't help it.

I saw a young boy walking nearby. I described Jim, and asked the boy if he'd seen anyone like him that day. The boy said Jim was at the farm of a man named Silas Phelps.

"That Jim was a runaway slave and now they've got him," the boy said. "There was a two hundred dollar reward for him. I saw the poster myself. Some old man gave away the information to the men in town for just forty dollars. It was like finding money on the road."

I sat on the raft and tried to figure out what to do next. I thought until my head was sore, but I couldn't see any way out of the trouble. After all we'd done for those scoundrels, everything was ruined because they were heartless enough to sell Jim out for forty dollars.

I thought I could write a letter back to Miss Watson. Maybe she would know what to do. Then I thought I would get in trouble for helping Jim escape and causing all of this trouble. I remembered all the good things Jim had done for me and how we helped and cared for each other. I knew that Jim would have to go back to his old life if I sent that letter. But if I could save him, he would be free again. Even if it meant that people thought I was doing a bad thing. I didn't care if people thought it was wrong. I was going to help him get free.

I hid the raft, the canoe, and all of our gear. Then I headed up toward the Phelps' farm. When I got there, it was all still and lonesome. It was a small cotton plantation with a rail fence around a two-acre yard and a big log house that had been whitewashed. As I walked toward the house, some dogs started barking. They didn't stop until a woman came outside. She was about forty-five or fifty years old. Two children and some slaves followed behind her. Everyone was smiling.

"It's *you* at last!" she said. "Am I right?"

"Yes, ma'am," I said, before I could even think about it.

She hugged me tightly and started crying. Then she told me that I didn't look like my mother, as she had expected.

"I'm so glad to see you!" she said. "Children, it's your cousin Tom! Come say hello. We thought you'd be here a few days ago. We were so worried."

I made up a story about my boat being

delayed. While we talked I tried to get information about who I was pretending to be. I also tried to find out anything I could about Jim. I guessed this woman was Mrs. Phelps. When she brought me into the house, I guessed that the man inside was Mr. Phelps.

"Why, who's this?" he asked when he saw me.

"Well, who do you think?" she said. "It's *Tom Sawyer!*"

CHAPTER 16

Tom Sawyer

∽

When I heard Tom's name, I almost fell over. But there was no time to think. They asked me all kinds of questions about Tom's family back home. I was so happy to know who I was supposed to be. I knew all the details and news of the Sawyer family. I talked and talked and gave them enough news for six Sawyer families. For example, I knew right away that the old woman who met me must have been his Aunt Sally. That meant the old man was his Uncle Silas.

I was feeling pretty comfortable being Tom

Sawyer, but then I thought, suppose Tom comes down that road just like I did? And suppose he tells them who I am before I can give him a signal to keep quiet? I couldn't have that, so I told the folks that I was going into town to fetch my luggage. When I was halfway there, sure enough, there was Tom Sawyer coming my way. I called out to him and he stopped, his mouth open like a trunk. He thought I was a ghost.

"I never did you any harm," he said. "Why would you want to come back and haunt me?"

"I haven't come back. I was never gone," I said.

It took some explaining before Tom understood my situation. Then he was excited. He loved adventures. I told him all about the two frauds and how Jim had been captured. I said that my plan was to pretend to be Tom until I could find a way to free Jim. I also wanted to be sure that I was well away from the duke and the king.

Tom said he knew exactly what to do. First, I

went back to the Phelps' farm with his luggage. Then Tom came along about a half hour after. He pretended to be his own brother, Sid.

"Why, dear me, this is such a surprise," said Aunt Sally. "We weren't expecting you, only Tom. Sis never wrote to me about anybody coming but him."

"I wasn't supposed to come, but I begged and begged and at the last minute she let me go," he said.

We had dinner then. Tom and I tried to find out some news about Jim, but we couldn't learn anything. Then Tom mentioned seeing a poster for a show in town and asked if we could go. Uncle Silas said no, but I realized it was the show that the duke and the king were doing. That night I told Tom about the show. We decided to sneak out to warn the townspeople about those two frauds.

When we got into town that night, we saw a rush of people in the street. They were all carrying torches. Everyone was yelling and whooping, banging tin pans, and blowing horns. We got out of their way as fast as we could. As they passed we saw the king and the duke. They were covered in tar and feathers, and sitting on an old train rail being carried by the crowd. I knew it was them, even though they were covered with tar and feathers. I felt sorry for them. I didn't think I could be angry with them anymore. It was a terrible thing to see. Human beings can be awfully cruel to one another.

CHAPTER 17

Saving Jim

ᥫᬒ

The next day, Tom told me that he'd seen one of the slaves bringing some food to a little hut some distance away from the house. I had seen him, too, and Tom said Jim might be in there. Tom said the slave had unlocked the door to the hut with a key that Uncle Silas carried. Well right away I thought we should steal the key that night and set Jim free. But Tom had other ideas.

"That would certainly work," he said. "But it's too darn simple. There's nothing *to* it."

I knew Tom would have his own plans. I also knew that they would be difficult and dangerous, and he would probably change them ten times a minute. And that's what he did. He wanted to set Jim free, but he had to do it his own way.

We went to the hut that night. There was a hole on one side that I thought Jim could climb through if we could tear off one of the boards.

"I should hope we can find a way that's a little more complicated that *that*," Tom said. "Something mysterious and troublesome and good."

We found some tools, which delighted Tom.

"We'll *dig* him out," he said. "It'll take about a week! It's perfect."

The next day we followed the slave who was bringing food out to the hut. After a lot of talking, we convinced him to let us see inside. It was dark, but Jim was there. He was sitting on a flimsy bed, leaning up against the wall; he looked sad.

"Why, *Huck!* My goodness, is that Tom Sawyer?" Jim said.

We said we were going to set him free and that he shouldn't worry if he heard any digging at night. It was just us. Jim only had time to hold each of us by the hand and thank us. Then we had to leave before the slave who had brought the food came looking for us.

It didn't take long for Tom to start changing his plan. He decided it was just too easy to dig Jim out of the hut. Jim needed a rope ladder, and he had to write letters about how lonely he felt. Tom had many ideas like these, which he had picked up from all the adventure stories he read.

We started digging under the hut that night after everyone went to sleep. At first Tom wanted us to dig with our hands, but that was

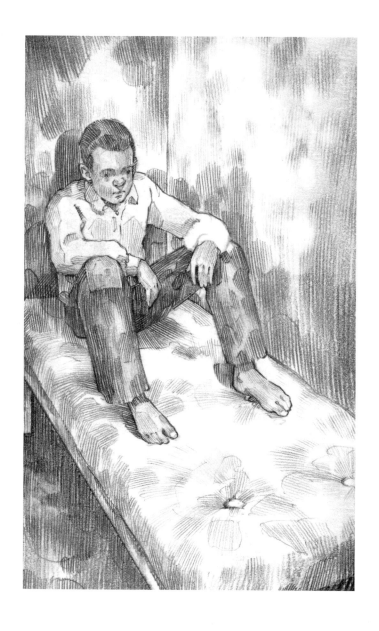

taking too long. Finally he said it would probably be all right for us to use the picks and shovels we had borrowed. We dug until we were too tired to continue. The hole was just deep enough to crawl under the wall of the hut and get inside.

The next day we borrowed a sheet for Jim to write on. We also brought Jim some spoons and a candlestick that he could use to make a pen. We took some candles and plates, and other things that Tom thought would be useful.

That night we crawled into the hut and woke Jim. He was so happy to see us that he almost cried. He wanted to leave with us right away, but Tom explained how that wasn't the right way to do things. He said we had to save Jim according to all the adventure stories. Well Tom was the expert on that, so Jim and I went along with him. Tom explained how Jim should write on the sheet and the plates, and told him how to make the rope ladder. It was all very confusing, but Jim said he would try to do it all. Tom was in high spirits. He said it was the best fun he ever had in his life.

CHAPTER 18

Tom's Adventure

⌒

Over the next few days, Aunt Sally and Uncle Silas began to notice that items were missing from the house: the sheet, spoon, candles, and other things that Tom had decided were necessary to free Jim. Tom and I tried to fool them by replacing some of the items and taking others later on.

Tom's plan was also bothering Jim, who was supposed to write poems and paint a coat of arms. The problem was that none of us knew how to do that. Tom did a pretty good job of making them up for Jim. Three weeks passed. I thought it was taking a very long time to free him.

When we were finally ready to set Jim free, Tom said we had to write warning letters to Aunt Sally and Uncle Silas. The letters had to be from a mysterious stranger. Tom had read all about it in one of his books. One night he left a note that said:

"Beware. Trouble is brewing. Keep a sharp lookout. *Unknown Friend.*"

He slipped it under the front door of the house. The next night he drew a skull and cross-bones on the front door. The night after that he drew a coffin on the back door. It was all very mysterious and scary. Aunt Sally and Uncle Silas were quite upset. The slightest noise outside made them jump. People thought there were ghosts everywhere.

Then Tom left another letter:

"I wish to be your friend. I want to warn you that there is a desperate gang who want to steal the runaway slave tonight. They have been trying to scare you so you will stay in the house and not bother them. I am one of the gang, but I wish to quit it and live an honest life again."

The letter said the gang would sneak onto the farm at midnight and told how the family could capture the gang.

The next day while Tom was out making preparations, I went back to the house. There was quite a crowd there! Fifteen farmers and every one of them had a weapon. I felt sick. Everyone was talking in a low voice. They all looked fidgety and uneasy. I ran and found Tom at the hut as soon as I could get away. I told him about the men.

His eyes blazed and he said:

"No! Is that so! *Ain't* that something!"

"Hurry!" I said. "We have to set Jim free now."

We slipped the chain off Jim's leg. Just then we heard the men approaching. We all hid when they opened the door. It was dark and no one saw us as we crawled out of the hole we had dug. We crept around outside toward the fence and were nearly away when Tom's pants caught on a piece of wood. Someone heard us and yelled:

"Who's that? Answer or I'll shoot!"

We didn't answer. We just ran and ran. There was a *bang, bang, bang*! and the bullets whizzed around us! We heard the men yell:

"There they are! They're headed for the river! After them, boys, and turn loose the dogs!"

We made it to the river and found where I had hidden my canoe. We hopped in and rowed for dear life toward the island where I had hidden the raft. We were far away from the men. When we finally stepped onto the raft, I said:

"Now Jim, you're free again. I bet you'll never be a slave again."

"It was a mighty good job, too, Huck," he said. "It was planned beautifully. Nobody could have come up with a better plan than that."

We were all as glad as we could be, but Tom was even happier because he had a bullet in the calf of his leg. Well Jim and I didn't feel as good as we did before. It was hurting Tom a lot and bleeding pretty heavily. We tore up one of the duke's shirts to bandage him, but he wanted to do it himself.

"We did it so elegantly, didn't we?" he said, still excited about the escape.

Jim and I knew Tom needed a doctor, but Tom didn't want one. It never happened like that in any of his adventure books. Finally he agreed to let me go. He didn't have a choice, but I let him think it was his decision. He made me promise to blindfold the doctor so he wouldn't know where we were hidden. I said I would and Jim said he would hide until the doctor left.

The doctor I found in town was a very kind-looking old man. I told him my brother was hurt in a hunting accident and that we wanted him to help us without telling our parents.

"Who are your folks?" he asked.

"The Phelpses."

"Oh," he said, and a few moments later: "How did you say he got shot?"

"He had a dream and it shot him."

"Some dream," he said.

When he saw my canoe, he said it wouldn't be big enough for both of us. He told me to stay at his office until he came back. I didn't have time to argue with him, so I told him which island Tom was on and he set out for it.

Well pretty soon I fell asleep out there. When I woke up the sun was high. I went to the doctor's house, but they told me he wasn't back yet. I thought that sounded pretty bad for Tom. I wanted to get back to the island right away. I left the doctor's house, but just as I turned the corner I bumped right into Uncle Silas!

"Why, *Tom*! Where have you been all this time, you rascal?"

"I haven't been anywhere," I said. "Just hunting for that runaway slave, me and Sid."

"Why, wherever did you go? Your aunt's been mighty worried."

"We were all right," I said. "We followed the men and dogs and took a canoe out onto the water. We got a little lost and slept out there until just now. Sid's at the post office. We were about to head home."

Uncle Silas came with me to the post office to "get" Sid. Of course, he wasn't there, so Uncle Silas said we should head home right away. He picked up a letter that had come in for him and then we left.

When we got home, Aunt Sally was so glad to see me that she laughed and cried and hugged me. She was pretty angry, too, and said she would also be angry with Sid as soon as he came home.

The place was full of farmers and their families. Everybody was talking about the excitement of the previous night and the mysterious letters and drawings. I knew these had all been done by Tom and me, but I kept my mouth shut.

Tom didn't some back at all that day. Uncle Silas went into town several times to look for him and by nightfall he and Aunt Sally were very worried. She stayed up all night waiting for him. Uncle Silas was out again before breakfast, but he couldn't find any trace of Tom. When he came back, he remembered the letter he had picked up the previous day. He gave it to Aunt Sally and she said:

"Why, it's from St. Petersburg. It's from Sis."

But before she could open it, she dropped it and ran to the door. She had seen something outside. So had I. It was Tom Sawyer on a mattress, the old doctor, and Jim, who had his hands tied behind him. A lot of people were walking behind them.

She started crying and hugged Tom. He was very tired and couldn't speak. She and Uncle Silas were so happy to see that Tom was alive. A few of the people brought Tom upstairs. I followed the crowd of people who took Jim away. They thought he was responsible for all the trouble last night and were very mad at him. He didn't say anything and pretended not to recognize me. They took him to the same hut as before, but this time they chained him up a lot more and had guards stand outside. They were pretty hard on him until the doctor told everyone to treat Jim well.

"When I found the boy I was able to fix the wound easily enough, but he was in no condition for me to leave to get help. He got a worse and worse and talked all sorts of foolishness. I said I had to get help for him. As soon as I said it, that runaway slave came out from wherever he was hiding and said he would help. He did, too, and very well. He helped me care for the boy until we saw some men pass by in a boat on the river. He let them tie up his hands and never made a fuss as we brought him and the boy back home. He's not a bad man, gentlemen."

That softened up a lot of the people. I was thankful to that old doctor for doing Jim such a good turn. The men agreed that Jim had done well and they took off many of his chains.

CHAPTER 19

The End of the Tale

By the next morning, Tom was feeling a good deal better. He woke up while Aunt Sally and I were in his room.

"Why, I'm home!" he said, looking at me. "How's that? Where's the raft?"

"It's all right," I said.

"And Jim?"

"The same," I said, but it was pretty hard to talk with Aunt Sally in the room.

"Good! Splendid! *Now* we're all right and safe! Did you tell Aunty?"

I was going to say yes, but she interrupted and said, "About what, Sid?"

"Why, about the way the whole thing was done."

"What whole thing?"

"Why, *the* whole thing: how Tom and I set the runaway slave free."

"My goodness, what *is* this child talking about?"

"We *did* set him free, me and Tom. We planned it all and we *did* it. We did it elegantly, too."

Then he told her about our weeks of planning, how we took all those items from the house and left the letters and drawings, and how the men had chased and shot at us.

"Well, I've never heard anything like it," she said. "So it was *you,* you little rascals. You were the ones who made all the trouble and scared everyone so much."

She was very angry, but Tom was so proud and

joyful that he just couldn't contain his happiness. Of course, he wasn't so happy when he learned that Jim wasn't free anymore. He sat up in bed and demanded that they set Jim free.

"He's as free as anyone else," he said.

"What are you talking about?"

"I've known him all my life and so has Tom. Old Miss Watson died two months ago. After Jim left, she felt terrible about wanting to sell him. She set him free in her will!"

"Why on earth did you go through all that effort to help him escape if you knew he was already free?"

"For the *adventure* of it, of course!" he said. Then he stared at the door and said, "Aunt Polly!"

And there she stood, looking as sweet and friendly as an angel. Aunt Sally ran to her and they hugged and cried. I crawled under the bed. Aunt Polly said hello to Tom and Aunt Sally said:

"That isn't Tom, it's Sid. Tom was here just a moment ago. Where is he now?"

"You mean where is Huck Finn," said Aunt Polly, and she told me to come out from under the bed.

Well it all came out then. Aunt Polly told her sister and Uncle Silas about me. The letter that Aunt Sally had been about to read before Tom came back was from Aunt Polly. She was writing to tell them that she was coming to visit. She had heard that Tom and Sid were both here. She knew Sid was back at home, so she wanted to see what was really happening.

We had Jim out of his chains in no time. When Aunt Polly, Aunt Sally, and Uncle Silas learned how much Jim had helped the doctor with Tom, they made a great fuss over him. They gave him all he wanted to eat and a good place to stay.

Tom, Jim, and I talked a great deal about

having some more adventures together, but I said I wouldn't be able to go along because I didn't have any money left. My pap must have taken it all from Judge Thatcher by now.

"No he hasn't," Tom said. "It's all there. Your pap hasn't been back since you left. At least, he hadn't been when I left town."

Jim looked very serious just then and said:

"He's not coming back any more, Huck."

"Why Jim?" I asked.

He didn't want to say anything, but I insisted and he finally told me.

"Do you remember that house we saw floating down the river with a dead man inside? Remember how I looked at him but I wouldn't let you come in to see? Well, you can get your money when you want it, because that man was your pap."

Tom's almost healed now and there isn't much more to write about. I'm happy about that. If I would have known how hard it was to write a book, I wouldn't have started. And I won't do any more of it.

I think I might head out again soon, though. Aunt Sally says she's going to adopt me and civilize me. I can't stand that. I've been there before.

What Do *You* Think?
Questions for Discussion

❦

Have you ever been around a toddler who keeps asking the question "Why?" Does your teacher call on you in class with questions from your homework? Do your parents ask you questions about your day at the dinner table? We are always surrounded by questions that need a specific response. But is it possible to have a question with no right answer?

The following questions are about the book you just read. But this is not a quiz! They are designed to help you look at the people, places, and events in the story from different angles. These questions do not have specific answers. Instead, they might make you think of the story in a completely new way.

Think carefully about each question and enjoy discovering more about this classic story.

1. Throughout the book, Huck is forced to pretend to be many other people. Have you ever pretended to be someone else? Who?

2. When Tom comes for Huck, he signals to him by meowing. Why do you think they picked this sound? Have you and your friends ever had a secret sound or password that only you knew?

3. Huck finally escapes from his father by tricking everyone into thinking he has died. Were you surprised by his plan? Have you ever tricked anyone into believing something that wasn't true?

4. Huck and Jim have different reasons for running away. Do you think one is more

important than the other? Have you ever tried to run away?

5. Huck says there is "no home like a raft." Do you agree? If you could live anywhere, where would you pick?

6. Were you surprised that Miss Sophia ran off with Harney Shepherdson? Do you think Huck should have told someone about the note in the Bible? Have you ever kept a secret with disastrous results?

7. Huck has a strong sense of responsibility. Why do you think he felt responsible for the battle between the Shepherdsons and the Grangerfords? Have you ever felt responsible for something that wasn't your fault?

8. Huck mentions that the king and the duke will be tarred and feathered as a punishment. What do you think this means? What is the worst punishment you ever received?

9. Huck seems to live by his own code. What do you think his code is? Do you have a code that you live by?

10. Who do you think is smarter: Tom or Huck? Who do you think is more practical? Which of these characters are you more like?

Afterword

by Arthur Pober, EdD

✂

First impressions are important.

Whether we are meeting new people, going to new places, or picking up a book unknown to us, first impressions count for a lot. They can lead to warm, lasting memories or can make us shy away from any future encounters.

Can you recall your own first impressions and earliest memories of reading the classics?

Do you remember wading through pages and pages of text to prepare for an exam? Or were you the child who hid under the blanket to read with a flashlight, joining forces with Robin Hood to save Maid Marian? Do you remember only how long it took you to read a lengthy novel such as *Little Women*? Or did you become best friends with the March sisters?

Even for a gifted young reader, getting through long chapters with dense language can easily become overwhelming and can obscure the richness of the story and its characters. Reading an abridged, newly crafted version of a classic novel can be the gentle introduction a child needs to explore the characters and story line without the frustration of difficult vocabulary and complex themes.

Reading an abridged version of a classic novel gives the young reader a sense of independence and the satisfaction of finishing a "grown-up" book. And when a child is engaged with and inspired by a classic story, the tone is set for further exploration of the story's themes, characters, history, and details. As a child's reading skills advance, the desire to tackle the original, unabridged version of the story will naturally emerge.

If made accessible to young readers, these stories can become invaluable tools for understanding themselves in the context of their families and social environments. This is why the *Classic Starts* series includes questions that stimulate discussion regarding the impact and social relevance of the characters and stories today. These questions can foster lively conversations between children and their parents or teachers. When we look at the issues, values, and standards of past times in terms of how we live now, we can appreciate literature's classic tales in a very personal and engaging way.

Share your love of reading the classics with a young child, and introduce an imaginary world real enough to last a lifetime.

Dr. Arthur Pober, EdD

Dr. Arthur Pober has spent more than twenty years in the fields of early-childhood and gifted education. He is the former principal of one of the world's oldest laboratory schools for gifted youngsters, Hunter College Elementary School, and former Director of Magnet Schools for the Gifted and Talented for more than 25,000 youngsters in New York City.

Dr. Pober is a recognized authority in the areas of media and child protection and is currently the U.S. representative to the European Institute for the Media and European Advertising Standards Alliance.

Explore these wonderful stories in our
Classic Starts™ library.